I0607021

Charles L. Paige

The White Shoshone

Charles L. Paige

The White Shoshone

ISBN/EAN: 9783743388581

Manufactured in Europe, USA, Canada, Australia, Japa

Cover: Foto ©Andreas Hilbeck / pixelio.de

Manufactured and distributed by brebook publishing software
(www.brebook.com)

Charles L. Paige

The White Shoshone

THE WHITE SHOSHONÉ

BY

✳

AUTHOR'S EDITION

SAN FRANCISCO
THE BANCROFT COMPANY
1890

Copyright, 1890
by
CHARLES L. PAIGE

'TIS only a quaint tradition
        In broken accents told—
'Twill scarcely bear rendition
        By mortal, over-bold ;
No white man's heart can know it,
        No Indian e'er will tell—
The valleys will not show it,
        Nor the mountains break the spell.

The stream will not reveal it,
        It runs so fast and strong—
The lake will still conceal it
        And keep its secret long ;
'Tis gone, and gone forever !
        An atom on the blast—
Or a wave of the Sinking river,
        Into the silent past !

But an old, old man remembers,
        And feebly tries to speak,
Points to the dying embers—
        To his wrinkled brow and cheek ;
To the mountain hoar and tawny,
        To the withered Autumn leaf—
The tale of the White Shoshoné,
        The tale of the mystic chief.

If these things were, then this true record is—
If they were not—why, then, here's something new.

—*Fugitive Thoughts*

THE WHITE SHOSHONÉ

❊

CHAPTER I

I

'TWAS years, long years ago, as far away
　　As wrinkled age from childhood seems :
The Indian 's very old when bent and gray,
　　The past to him a maze of dreams,
Yet, steady flames are kindled from a spark,
And bright the fire that flashes from the dark.

II

Long, long before the white men came, said he—
　　When he was young, long time ago ;
A man was very old, who scarce could see ;
　　A hundred years?　He did not know—
Perhaps much more ; all were Shoshonés then,
With many wigwams, and the braves were men.

III

And all the valleys, far as could be seen,
　　Far as the mountains blue and dim,
Waved with tall grass, a rolling sea of green ;
　　The river, sparkling to the brim,
For miles and miles, like silver wound the river,
To where it makes the lake and sinks forever.

IV

There were no houses, stores or wagons then—-
    The fish were plenty, deer were tame,
More antelope, more buffaloes than men—
    And every year was just the same ;
The summers and the winters passed away,
And no one counted them or named each day.

V

There were no fences, no man owned the land,
    Or on one spot would live and die ;
No towns were ever built to always stand,
    No roof to always hide the sky ;
A hundred lodges yesterday were there,
To-day were gone, the stranger knew not where.

VI

In summer to the mountains far away—
    In winter to the plains below ;
No Indian here or there will always stay,
    In summer's heat and winter's snow ;
The world is wide and no one spot complete,
Except for men who only work and eat.

VII

The white men live in houses all the year,
    Work hard for money, read, keep store—
The Indian out of doors, just like the deer
    Has earth and sky and asks no more ;
Nor knows to-day of past or future sorrow,
The past is gone, there may be no to-morrow

VIII

There are too many men and some must go,
　　The Indians first to other land ;
The great Shoshoné Chief had told them so—
　　Against the sun had waved his hand,
And shook his head, and told that all would be
Just as it is, and all old men would see.

IX

He saw so very far, he always knew,
　　Yet spoke but little, softly, slow—
And everything he said was always true,
　　His nod was yes, his silence, no ;
When he was quiet all the camps were still,
He raised his hand, it signaled every hill.

X

In council he spoke well, his words were few,
　　But old men bowed, and braves were still—
For come what might, he knew just what to do
　　On the wide plain, or highest hill ;
Let sickness come, or danger, want or war
The word came first to him from near or far.

XI

Where e'er his lodge was set there many came,
　　Though long the trail, 'twas never dim—
For where he went was always found the game,
　　And the Great Spirit guided him ;
Let the long winter come with snow and storm,
No one was hungry, every wigwam warm.

XII

But, he is gone! and with him many a brave!
　　Their fires are out, their lodges, where?
On the Black Mountain still the cedars wave—
　　Too sadly wave,—they are not there;
See, in the valley, houses everywhere—
But not a wigwam, Malo is not there.

XIII

Yet the thin smoke from Indian fires you see,
　　Here in the hills, yes, some are here!
Some boys, some squaws and some old men like me,
　　With faces red, but hearts of deer!
Where are the warriors, where is Malo?　Why
Do white men come so fast and Indians die!

XIV

Ugh!　He spoke well!　He knew, long years ago,
　　He waved his hand and shook his head—
Pointed far off to the white peaks and snow,
　　We knew his sorrow but not all he said;
Why did he go?　And will he always ride,
Before the wind and storm, to always hide?

XV

We see him in the mornings, on the plain—
　　Ride through the shadowy mountains there;
See warriors follow, come, and go again—
　　But with the sun all goes to air!
Fast o'er the frozen snow, before the gale
He rides, they follow fast, we find no trail.

XVI

And the white sequaw with the yellow hair,
    Pale and afraid, eyes like the sun;
White? White like the chief but soft and fair,
    Does she now listen, is she won?
Malo was strong and brave, his words were wise,
But ah! He looked too deep into her eyes.

XVII

Or does she flee and Malo yet pursue,
    The warriors following on, and on—
Far, far into the distant shadows blue,
    Or through the mystic hills at dawn?
It may be they live where the river goes,
Deep underneath the mountains, no one knows.

XVIII

Somewhere they are—a thousand lodges are—
    Hosts of red faces, Indians all:
There the white maiden, like the brightest star,—
    There the great Malo, strong and tall!
There all the vanished herds, the fish and game,
With rivers, skies and mountains just the same.

XIX

Broad is the trail and trod by many feet,
    But all press forward on the track—
To some far place where sky and mountains meet,
    Not one, not ever one comes back!
Where leads the trail? Do none but white men know
Where is the land where only dead men go?

XX

Perhaps 'tis where so many suns have gone,
    In fire and gold beyond the land;
Or whence they come, in gold and fire at dawn,
    Across the world, none understand;
Where all the thousand moons, the stars shall stay
When they have left the skies and gone away.

XXI

Ugh?   Indians are not strong to read, or think,
    Their heads but full of things they see—
And the fierce water that the white men drink
    But staggers them, they fight or flee;
Yet thoughts they have and though they cannot know,
They wonder still that this, or that, is so.

XXII

Ah, in the time that was so long ago—
    Were many happier days than now;
Faint voices come on all the winds that blow,
    And bring thoughts back; we know not how
They come, faces long gone and vanished forms
Return with flying clouds, or whistling storms.

XXIII

He came across the mountains, o'er the sand,
    Which for long miles is dry and dead—
None saw him come, but first they saw him stand
    Beside his horse, with lifted head;
The great black horse, with iron upon his feet,
Limbs of the deer but stronger and more fleet!

CHAPTER II

I

BEFORE the sky was red at dawn he came—
Came close, too close for one alone;
Stranger and foe to us meant much the same
Who found no friends in men unknown!
Yet he stood there, so young, so white and tall—
Making no sign of fight or fear at all!

II

The braves sprang to their feet and quickly ran
To ponies grazing near the spot—
While dark eyes glanced to the great horse and man
Who saw them all but heeded not ;
The warriors gazed in wonder, but their eyes
Shone fiercely, anxious for the certain prize.

III

Some reached for arrows but no bow was bent,
The capture sure, none thought to kill ;
But forward, circling, watching as they went,
Sprang many men, the prize stood still !
The great horse, freed from saddle, ropes and rein
But raised his ears, and turned to graze again.

IV

The stranger laughed, as one who feared no harm—
Made signs of peace that Indians know—
While something gleamed and shone upon his arm
That was not spear, or knife or bow!
Straight to the fire he strode. The chief stood back
And signaled runners take the white man's track!

V

He quickly saw the sign and laughed again,
    Lifting one finger, shook his head—
Then waved his arm toward the open plain,
    Motioned for water, food and bed ;
At the chief's fire took venison from the poles,
Then, like the Indian, broiled it on the coals!

VI

All eyes were on the stranger, some admired
    While others gleamed with doubt or fear ;
He motioned to his feet, that he was tired—
    Then pointed far, where stood a deer,
He raised his rifle, aiming slow and true—
While all stood wondering what he meant to do—

VII

The flash of fire, the smoke, the sudden noise
    Were things not seen or heard before!
The startled warriors shouted, squaws and boys
    Ran off and could be seen no more!
The chief and others saw the deer's wild bound
And saw him fall, and struggling, tear the ground.

VIII

One brave, half doubting, started for the game,
    Oft glancing backward as he ran ;
Some followed cautiously, while others came
    And mutely gazed at gun and man :
Then, many speaking, questioned, it was queer
What made the noise and smoke, what killed the deer?

IX

No arrow half so far was ever sped
    With sound of thunder, fire and smoke;
The deer, yet warm, was brought but still and dead!
    Its red side showed the fatal stroke—
Ah, we've learned since the unseen leaden ball,
That makes men great to kill and conquer all.

X

Yes, all the tribes have learned it, one by one,
    Been driven back or killed like game ;
Shoshonés learned to dread the white man's gun,
    To fear its spiteful flash of flame!
They feared not men, where equal chance was given
They fought like men and not like squaws,were driven.

XI

The rifle is the ruler of the world—
    Speaking one word with deadly breath ;
Unseen but sure its fatal voice is hurled
    From fiery throat. Its one word, death—
Has cut the bow-strings of a host of braves,
Made warriors flee, or sent them to their graves.

XII

It was unfair! As helpless as the deer
    The Indian fell or starved; the gun
Has taken all the world and filled with fear
    The bravest hearts. All must be done
Just as the white man thinks; the earth is his,
Be thus, he says,—or die! and so it is.

XIII

It is not right, for different men were made
    And given mountains, lands and streams ;
Some plants are for the sun, some for the shade—
    Who thinks to change them only dreams ;
The mountains stand, the land stays always so—
The stream flows on, men only come and go.

XIV

Some day a mightier race of men will come,
    Take all your cities, hill and plain,
Claim the whole world and make of it a home,
    For savages and beasts again ;
Men can not always live on fiery drink—
Or stay in houses, work or read, or think.

XV

Ages ago, far southward, cities grew—
    Men builded them of solid stone,
Great towns were there, how many no one knew—
    They came and went, now all are gone ;
Huge piles of stone are there—high as yon hill—
The land is like the desert, dead and still.

XVI

Your race is rich and wise, why go so fast,
    Kill all the game, cut forests down,
Have roads of iron, great engines whizzing past—
    Spoil every valley with a town ?
Have crowds of strangers come and fill the land,
To work for pay, we did not understand.

XVII

Ah, he knew well ! He liked it not, but came
 Where much less troubled men could live,
Where life was quiet and the land was tame—
 None had to sell but all to give;
Chiefs then were great when brave, or strong or wise,
Not for big herds, broad lands or thinking eyes.

XVIII

He was an Indian, though his face was white
 His eyes not black, were deep and true ;
Spare, strong and tall he was, his step as light
 As mine was once, his hair dark, too—
Dark, straight and long like ours, we wondered then
From whence he came, from what strange tribe of
  men.

XIX

He saw all things and knew, but did not stare
 Not listening, yet he always heard ;
When any moved he knew why, how or where,
 Yet watched each rabbit, squirrel, bird.
Long by the fire he sat, some strange words said—
Then took chief Wahko's lodge and took his bed.

XX

He knew men well, great Wahko's eyes were bright,
 He saw each move the stranger made ;
Fierce he could be, and none more quick to fight,
 And when he spoke none disobeyed !
But now he only gazed, while, one by one
He had the stranger's saddle brought and gun.

XXI

These near the lodge were placed by careful hands,
  The great horse led to better feed ;
No doubt the stranger, bound for other lands
  Would soon awake and onward speed.
He was no foe, but some great chief unknown,
With mighty followers, though he seemed alone.

XXII

Long hours he slept while all the camp was stilled—
  Yet many talked, or watched or guessed—
Measured the distance where the deer was killed,
  Looked closely at its wounds when dressed ;
Eyed the queer gun, of polished steel and wood,
Horse, ropes and saddle, no one understood.

XXIII

Some took the trail and followed far the track
  Of the black horse, down to the plain—
There every trace was lost, and all came back,
  The moving sand made tracking vain ;
Of horse or man no further signs they found,
Though their shrewd eyes saw far, and read the
      ground.

XXIV

Runners to distant camps were sent, men came—
  But none had seen or heard of him ;
All much surprised, they wondered, talked the same,
  Whence could he come, unknown to them?
The horse was watched as if from him to learn,
But, from the camp his steps would never turn.

CHAPTER III

I

HEN he had fed, straight to the fire he
　　　went—
　　　Looked fierce, and snorted, stepped with care;
　　　Passed all the rest to stop at Wahko's tent
　　As if he knew his rider there!
With big bright eyes and shining coat he stood,
Heart, speed and strength for mountain, plain or flood.

II

In after time his mighty power was tried,
　　　Blood, strength and speed they failed not then—
When hardier steeds than him exhausted, died
　　　Urged to the last by desperate men!
They followed fast o'er desert, hill and plain
They followed far but never raced again!

III

Kosak they named him, horse with iron heart;
　　　Him none but two had e'er bestrode,
Across the plain he sped, swift as a dart—
　　　And faltered not with double load!
Where now is he? may not his tireless feet
Still skim the ground, as faithful, strong and fleet?

IV

The white chief came, and stroking Kosak's head,
　　　Placed on him saddle, rein and gun;
Then the great horse to wondering Wahko led—
　　　Where steel and silver caught the sun;
Made Kosak stand, then gave the chief his rein—
And walked away back to the fire again.

V

No words he spoke, but Wahko understood
    The stranger's sign to lodge and fire—
To mountain, valley, stream, to skins and food ;
    No words were needed, why inquire ?
He asked to stay, be friendly, hunt and fish—
And offered all he had to gain the wish.

VI

Wahko, the chief, much pleased, stood tall with pride,
    Marked well the horse, limbs, nostril, back—
His round bright eye, sharp ear, his glossy side,
    Broad breast, good feet and curving neck!
Looked close at gun and saddle, nothing said,
But doubtful what to say, he bowed his head.

VII

Then, to the stranger signed, that food and tent,
    Land, stream and camp like air was free ;
And leading Kosak here and there he went,
    Where some might touch and all could see!
Unsaddled then, the horse was left to stray,
Though many eyes were on him all that day.

VIII

Large skins and robes of fur were brought, soon
        placed,
    And a great lodge was made anew ;
Straight poles were set and all securely laced,
    With thongs and sinews woven through.
Water was brought in baskets, fish and game—
.Until like Wahko's lodge it seemed the same.

IX

Wahko, well pleased with all, yet often still;
   Eyed the white stranger where he moved ;
Saw with quick step and free he climbed the hill,
   Saw Kosak watching him he loved !
Enough, when the white chief awoke next day
Saddle and gun he found beside him lay.

X

And Wahko always followed close with him,
   Watching strange acts of skill or might,
His well-made dress of buckskin, strength of limb,
   Great horse and weapons, skin so white !
So sure he was to know, so quick to do,
And everything he said always so true.

XI

Some saw him watch for hours the herds of deer,
   The trees, the streams, the stars or sky—
Bring bits of rock and flowers from far and near,
   Do many things when none knew why ;
Fire from the sun he brought, or from his hand,
Caught fish and game when none could understand!

XII

Some doubted him and others felt in awe,
   Thinking his powers beyond belief ;
But injuring none and helping all, they saw
   How great he was, and called him chief ;
Malo, the great white chief ; the time was when
His word or sign could rouse a thousand men.

XIII

A thousand braves would come at sign or call,
    Each one to follow where he led ;
To hunt or fight, till the last man should fall ;
    They often murmured when he said,
That peace was wise, and brave men last to fight—
Cowards and curs the first to snarl and bite.

XIV

Across the world he said, men went to war
    And many brave men fought and fell ;
That thousands died, and sorrow spread afar—
    Though why they fought but fools could tell !
By making peace great warriors rose to fame,
Those making war were only known to shame !

XV

And so it was ; for many moons he stayed—
    Learned soon to understand and speak,
Till many dark-eyed boys grew less afraid,
    And many a maid less shy or meek;
Welcome he was to join in dance or game,
Which lasted always longer, if he came.

XVI

Sure traps were made for birds, for furs and fish
    Strange spears and barbs, unknown before—
Long coats of beaver skins, and none could wish,
    None knew, or thought, or cared for more ;
Great hunts there were, and Malo first to go,
Learned every trail through forest, sage and snow.

XVII

Sometimes to distant camps alone he went,
　Or rode with Wahko miles away,
Till known and welcome at the farthest tent—
　For days or months if he would stay ;
Sometimes, with many braves, he took the trail
If furs were needed or if food should fail.

XVIII

He always knew the best, no eye more true
　To follow track or guess the ground,
For buffalo, big sheep and deer he knew
　Where all herds moved, and soon were found;
Shrewd woho, fox, sly beaver, otter, mink
Like fools were caught if Malo cared to think.

XIX

But most he loved the camp, the fires by night,
　The sky and stars, or the great moon ;
The cries of wild-fowl, gathering for the flight,
　Of woho, wolf, coyote, coon—
His ear loved sounds, and understood the speech
Of all that lived, the joys or woes of each.

XX

He studied well the world, not men alone—
　No empty town or city here,
Built up with ugly houses, dead bare stone—
　To struggle for with toil and fear ;
The earth is full of life and man but one
Of many thousand things beneath the sun.

XXI

Men should have room or else their thoughts grow
    small ;
    In little space they hear and see
Few sounds and sights and think those few are all ;
    Men must have room, see far and free
'Twas thus he thought, but ah, her small pale face
Made him forget who might have saved a race !

XXII

Why not some other, many glanced at him—
    Wanama, blushing, walked away
When he was near ; and yet the eye was dim
    That could not see the wish to stay!
And fair she was, with graceful step and form,
Bright shining hair and eyes, red cheeks and warm.

XXIII

Soft furs and moccasins for him were made
    By skillful hands, and patient care,
With beads and feathers wrought which it was said—
    Wanama had been proud to wear ;
From him to her sometimes fine presents came,
But then, he gave to others just the same.

XXIV

One time when many came to feast and dance—
    When all the camp was full of men,
Some warriors came who found the fires by chance
    But, strangers all, they turned again
And soon were gone, save one alone who stayed,
Wounded and ill who trembled—much afraid.

CHAPTER IV

I

HIS breast was bleeding, but the wound was
    small,
    And many watched him try to speak,
Doubting the weakness of a man so tall—
    Yet always from his wound would break
A stream of blood ; when Malo came his eyes
Flashed quick with fear, with hatred and surprise.

II

Malo looked close, spoke fast and shook his head,
    Though the sick brave seemed not to hear—
Or understood him not ; then Malo said
    The brave would die. Not bow or spear
Had made the wound ; that nothing could be done,
And death would come before another sun.

III

An old man came who knew the stranger's tongue,
    Talked slow with him and heard him tell
How he, with twenty others, hunted long
    Far to the south ; that all went well
Until they saw a fire, two nights before—
Near the great falls where many waters roar.

IV

There they had gone at early dawn next day—
    Saw strange things there, by them not known;
Men with white faces motioned them away,
    Though they signed peace; one brave alone
Walked to their fire,—to him they sternly spoke !
He offered them his arrows, these they broke !

V

Then all the braves had stood away, quite far—
  And only looked, they had not seen
White men before ; they did not think of war!
  But only peace, and then between
Them and the fire a white man, tall and proud
Came, motioned them to go, spoke strong and loud.

VI

The warriors moved, but did not understand
  Why they should go, so stood again ;
Then the tall man with something in his hand
  Pointed to them across the plain ;—
Quick fires flashed !   Great noises, smoke, men fell !
Three fell to die! what killed them none could tell—

VII

All then was fear and mounting fast, they fled,—
  Save three, who not again would ride !
And as they rode, he felt his wound, which bled
  And pained him much ; they thought to hide,
Till looking back, they saw the white men fly
Swift as themselves; They stopped to question why.

VIII

The tents were moving, horses ran with them—
  Leaving the camp, they too showed fear!
Then he turned back, the braves all followed him—
  Strange men who killed then ran like deer !
Short council held, they had gone slowly back
And when dark came, they followed on the track.

IX

And as they rode their hearts grew fierce and hot,
    Till, late at night, the fire they found—
Of the strange men ; then they had questioned not
    But, creeping on, close to the ground,
They came quite near; then with fierce cries they rose,
Wild with revenge and hate and fought the foes !

X

The white men fought, but in the dark they fell—
    Seven men, none ran away he said;
He then grew sick and little more could tell,
    But that not all, not all were dead.
White sequaws, two there were; one hurt that day
Had died, one lived, and she they brought away.

XI

Six braves were killed, the others—gone and he
    Was dying fast, no more could speak;
Pointing to Malo, when he scarce could see,
    His eyes would flash ! then very weak—
He slept, to die; Malo was quickly gone,
Called Kosak, would have rode away alone,—

XII

So quick he was—and spoke so short and stern !
    But Wahko, with some twenty men
Rode fast with him, for never would he turn,
    But always ride; straight South, and then
Straight East; he well knew Kosak would not fail
Though dark it was, his feet would find the trail.

XIII

Malo was wrong but once, this time too fast—
    Too far he rode; he could not know
So dark it was! We swam the stream at last
    And crossed the valley, far too low.
The trail was kept high up above the plain
To see far off, but all eyes looked in vain.

XIV

On the wide plain no fire was seen, no spark
    O'er all the miles of sage and sand;
Wolves howled and wohos, hundreds in the dark—
    No other life in all the land;
No sounds of men, below it seemed but air
Around, beyond—and darkness everywhere.

XV

Long they rode on, or listening, looked for signs
    Of fires and men, but all were gone;
Till where the white cliffs stand, in broken lines,
    They stayed to rest and wait for dawn.
Here they had slept beneath the sky alone
On the small sage for beds, or chalky stone.

XVI

And then at dawn, far distant, men were seen,
    Who to the South and East rode fast;
Had crossed the valley higher up, between
    The camps and stream, where Malo passed!
All sought their horses, but there was but one,
And that one Kosak, all the others gone!

XVII

The tracks led to the lodges, miles away;
    The brave who watched had slept! Malo
Would ride alone, for none could make him stay—
    And they on foot must follow slow;
For horses one was sent, but he must run
And half the day be lost and high the sun !

XVIII

Malo rode fast, the great black horse ran free,
    But well his mighty tracks were known;
None, deep like his, did Wahko ever see—
    For days they stayed where sands had blown;
Across the plain with long, low bounds he sped
Straight for the East where all the sky was red.

XIX

Malo rode well, no warrior kept his place
    In easier form on the long ride;
Always o'er Kosak's ears he looked, his face,
    His breast, turned never once aside;
And Kosak knew, if some great leap he made
The leap was always sure and free his head !

XX

Malo rode far and soon beyond the sight
    Where sage or cedar grew was gone;
Then came the sun, and all the plain was bright—
    But Kosak's trail they followed on;
Wolves and coyotes ran, big herds of deer,
Or stayed to look, then ran again in fear.

XXI

The trail was reached where the strange braves had
      been—
    There Kosak's tracks, but not for long ;
He turned across the hills, ah, he had seen
    And knew their course. He might be wrong—
But no, the winding river, they must swim
He'd catch them there, the ford best known to him !

XXII

Should they all follow ? No, if horses came
    Time would be lost, and some must stay;
Ah, we were slow, he fast, always the same—
    No head was clear with him away.
When the low pass was reached, the sun was high—
There all stood still to look, with flashing eye:

XXIII

Men from the river rode, ten,—twelve,—one fled !
    And him all knew whose eyes could see ;
Malo it was, and Kosak,—fast he led
    While many followed ; swift was he !
He then long miles had run—now carried two,
Long miles must go, but ah, it seemed he flew !

XXIV

We could but stand ; no race was that for men—
    Though fleet of foot, the arrow might
Fly just as fast—but ne'er was seen again
    Through all the years, so swift a flight !
And then our ponies came, we chased the wind—
Rode fast and faster but rode far behind !

CHAPTER V

I

HY make so many words ? They caught
not him—
Their horses fell, we took them all
Horses and men. Ours stood with shaking
limb
But Kosak, white with foam, stood tall !
His blood soon cooled, his heart so strong and great
Beat slow and true, his sharp ears firm and straight.

II

The sequaw ?   She seemed dead, her face so pale, ·
In strange, soft dress, with yellow hair !
And Malo heard her heart, it did not fail,
She lived, he said, and he saw there
But only her ; his horse, the foes, the race—
Were all forgot, he only watched her face.

III

He only watched her face or took her hand,
Or spoke to her, who heard him not—.
And Kosak stood, made white with foam and sand
Proud still he was!   The fire still shot
From his bright eyes, while warriors stroked his
head—.
The sequaw ?   Ah, she wept, she was not dead.

IV

And Kosak—Ugh !   She only trembled, cried
She always trembled full of fear
And always clung to him, close to his side—
With beating heart, like the young deer.
She trusted only him, Wanama came
And they grew friends but never just the same.

V

Lolak, they named her, she with yellow hair—
　　They loved her too in after days,
So kind she was, afraid, so still and fair,
　　Yet never understood their ways.
She feared them all but hundreds would have fought
For him, for her, and yet she saw it not.

VI

Her foes would all have died, fast bound were they ;
　　And yet she sent them food and drink—
Malo unbound them, let them ride away—
　　But ah, he gave them much to think !
They all were brought, then standing with his gun
He waved his hand, they saw the setting sun.

VII

Each one with folded arms but thought to die
　　And looked to him, to sun and plain ;
At him with hate and steady flashing eye—
　　Not one feared death or thought of pain.
Horses were brought and to each wondering brave
A horse was led, to each a rein he gave.

VIII

He waved his hand again, their eyes gleamed still,
　　But, when they understood to go—
Each looked again to sun, to camp and hill—
　　And wondered much, their thoughts were slow,
Then slow they rode, taking the eastward track—
The horses after many days came back.

Malo went southward far, dead men were there
    Men with white faces, all were found;—
Eight graves were made,—she with the yellow hair
    Knew then, now white men know the ground.
Wagons and guns were there, all else was brought
To her; for days she only cried and thought.

Then winter came and the great camp was made
    With many wigwams, lodges, men,
Dried grasses piled for Kosak, close he stayed,
    When snow fell deep; the ponies then
Knew where to range and where was best to go—
Kosak feared naught but winter's ice and snow.

He suffered not ; shelter for him was spread,
    And by his tent great fires were kept ;
Lolak ?—None wanted food or furs or bed
    By Wanama she lived and slept ;
A lodge was made of fur, close from the storm—
Your houses all are cold, her lodge was warm.

Malo saw none but her, if she were by,
    And heard no sound when she should speak,
But her low voice, with ever watching eye
    He guarded her ! Why ? She was weak—
She feared all things ; she wept ; she could not run
Swift like Wanama, strong in cold or sun.

XIII

The air was full of silver while she sung
    Strange songs, that Indians laughed to hear—
Yet listened close ; great Kosak knew her tongue
    And came to stand with pointed ear,
As if he understood ; perhaps 'twas so—
There are so many things that none can know.

XIV

When warmer suns had come, and snows had gone,
    Kosak was hers to pet or ride ;
Well she could ride and far, sometimes alone
    She thought she rode none by her side—
But keen eyes watched from rocks, or bush, or hill,
Or friendly shadows followed sure and still.

XV

To any wish she had no one said no :
    Had finest feathers, beads and furs—
She looked to mountain, there the camps would go ;
    She saw the valley, it was hers,
Pet fawns for her, and rabbits, Malo caught
Ravens and birds, for her alone he thought.

XVI

And all long days he laughed when she was glad
    Made boats for her at every stream;
Or, he was silent if she would be sad;
    If she spoke not, he did but dream.
Then many times she wept, why, none could tell
And listened not, though Malo spoke so well.

XVII

It takes so many words, much time to say
    So many things; The summer came
But ah, so long ago, so far away !
    And nothing now is left the same.
The mountains stand but all the fires are gone,
The trails all dim, the lodges few and lone.

XVIII

Hundreds of moons ago it was; men spoke
    Again of white men to the East;
Great councils then were held, big fires, much smoke
    Much talk, with dance and feast !
Malo heard all who came, sent runners far
And counseled always peace, no war.

XIX

Fires flashed by night from every mountain top,
    Or smokes by day, of watching men;
Then would be quiet, signals too would stop
    Then runners come, fires flash again !
Strange stories then flew fast from mouth to mouth—
Of men and wagons seen far to the South !

XX

The camps were moved ; ah, she would have it so !
    He waved his hand but shook his head—
Pointed to westward, to the peaks and snow,
    Spoke long to her; the words he said
None knew yet she would always stand
Look South, and point her small white hand.

XXI

She liked not us, the land, she loved not him—
     And yet, were any sick, she brought
The choicest food, did all she could for them ;
     Great medicine failed if she came not :
To him would kindly speak and smile to him—
And then would weep, her big bright eyes be dim.

XXII

Did any die her tears would always fall,
     And yet, she counseled not to weep;
Somewhere, she said, they lived, each one and all
     And were not lost and did but sleep:
We did not understand, she did not know—
She might have always stayed, why should she go ?

XXIII

He knew all things and asked her still to stay,
     But showed her fires across the plain ;
Had Kosak brought, and with her rode away—
     Then he alone came back again !
Too sad he was, his lodge no more his home;—
Long days he watched, and Kosak did not come.

XXIV

Great fires he always made and kept them bright
     Had warriors ride and watch the land,—
Till, westward far, was seen a double light,
     And then he seemed to understand,
And ever then, with Wahko, fast would ride
Long hours in silence.   Friends and side by side.

CHAPTER VI

I

AND warriors followed then, great herds they
found
   Much game was killed ; it pleased him not;
The mighty gun was still, its sure sharp
sound
Was heard no more, no more was sought;
Strong bows his arm could bend, his arrows fly
Swift, far and sure—and yet he would not try.

II

True friend he was, always so wise and brave ;
   And Wahko followed close with him ;
Why should he weep when with strong hand he gave,
   The silver bow ?   Why his clear eye be dim ?
Wahko was great, few men who did not know,
The mighty chief, him of the Silver bow !

III

A hundred fires went out, his tribe grew small ;
   Lodges went South, his bravest men—
To South and East, his warriors strong and tall,
   And few, so few, returned again !
Had Malo stayed wise council would have won,
And no fierce battle been, there—to the sun.

IV

Kosak came back, again at dawn he came—
   No rider, saddle, rope, or rein !
But only him, the great horse, just the same ;
   And Malo found, beneath his mane,
The speaking paper, long and close he read,
Then placed it by his heart and shook his head.

V

And Kosak always watched, he might have spoke—
    His head so close to Malo's kept ;
And all the night he stood, or sniffed the smoke,
    Or ever near his fire he stepped.
Kind hands there were to stroke him, soft ones too,
But he would look and sigh as if he knew !

VI

Where had he been, they wondered ; ah, so long—
    Far to the South and West somewhere ;
He could not tell, yet he was brave and strong,
    Had suffered not.   Had she stayed there?
Or where was she? and were there thousands, all
With faces white, so fair, or great and tall ?

VII

Ah, then days came and past, so soon were gone !
    And he, with twenty warriors, went
To South and West, left Wahko's heart a stone—
    So sad it was !   His silent tent
Still stood ; and Wahko must not fail
To keep bright fires ! Ah, whither wound the trail ?

VIII

Where wound the trail so narrow that his friend,
    Might not, as always, with him ride ?
Why, he would follow, if, at some sharp bend,
    There was no room to keep his side !
But he said always no, and shook his head,—
And westward rode when all the sky was red.

IX

Bright fires were kept when rain might come or
    snow—
    They always burned ; he never came !
A hundred fires went out but Silver Bow
    Still kept some bright, always the same ;
Young boys grew men and men grew still and cold—
He did not come ; yet Wahko was so old !

X

White men ?   Ah, yes, so many hundreds ! all
    Like him are white, some strong and straight ;
They have no hearts like his, their's all are small
    And quick to fill with fire and hate !
Their eyes are bright, but never one sees clear—
They chilled the Indian's blood and made him fear.

XI

They only saw his furs, his sequaws, lands—
    Killed all the game or made it flee ;
Spoke all with double tongue ! Their grasping hands
    Held not their hearts, but rifles ; see !
See all the fences, houses, stores and men,—
And always strangers come and go again.

XII

And they hunt cattle, gold or work and read,
    Or buy and sell with money ; they
Give Indians money, then they make them need—
    And take it back again, and say,
That all is theirs, they bought it ; then they fight !
The Indian's always wrong and they are right.

XIII

And so it is ; they claim no more their own
    But try to live, and all are sad ;
Some day no lodge will stand, not one alone—
    And men will speak all Indians bad ;
But then—perhaps there is a land somewhere,
Where only Indians live, none others there.

XIV

Or he will come, sometime, at dawn again—
    Will wave his hand, great hosts arise !
And then the fires will burn on hill and plain,
    And Kosak come with blazing eyes !
Lodges on every side will be, great braves—
Thousands of Indians ; nowhere any graves.

XV

Ah, he still lives, we see him often ride :
    They are not shadows at the dawn !
And many follow him ; they do not hide,
    But watch and ride forever on ;
Some day he's sure to come and wave his hand,—
All will be changed and men will understand.

XVI

Ah, so !   He may be dead, but Chief Wahko
    Yet lives, a bent old man he seems ;
None call him chief, and he of the Silver Bow
    Speaks brokenly, they think he dreams !
He sees not clear, his poor old eyes are dim;—
—White men call him roughly, old Indian Jim.